TRICK OR TWEET

Trick or Tweet

Jadie's Halloween Costume

Jo Gonsalves

A Dr. Jo Story

To my grandchildren,
my muses for mischief-making.
- Dr. Jo

"Gee Whiz!" said Mom. "Halloween is almost here, and we do not have our costumes yet. I need to think of something quick. We cannot go to school on Halloween without our costumes, Jadie."

"What is Halloween?" I wondered.

Mom smiled. "You are going to love Halloween, Jadie. All the teachers and students wear costumes to school. It is so much fun!"

"Hmm," Mom said. "This could be a bit tricky. What kind of costume should you wear? I have many costumes in my closet, but none of them will fit a little parrot. Let's check online," she said. I was excited to see all the parrot costumes!

I sat on her shoulder while Mom opened her laptop.

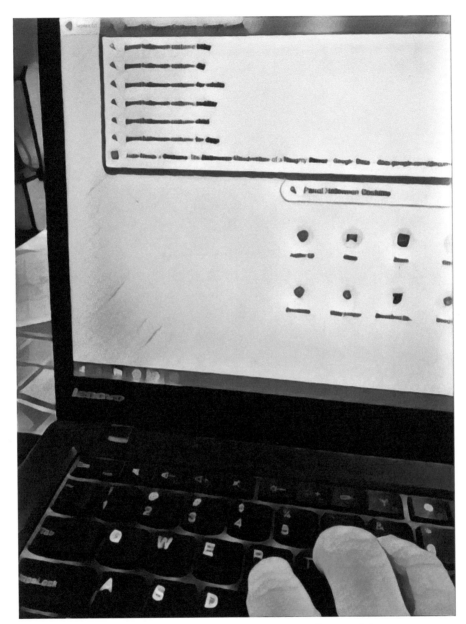

Mom typed "Parrot Halloween Costume" in the search bar.

"Oh dear," Mom said, when she saw the picture on the screen. "This is all wrong."

"This is NOT a Halloween costume for a parrot, Jadie. This is a Halloween parrot costume for a human. What are we going to do?"

"Do not worry, Mom," I thought. "You always manage to think of something."

Mom thought and thought...

"Hmm," she said. "I think I can make you a costume."

Mom thought some more...

"How about if I take one of Grandpy's old green socks and make you a cute green caterpillar costume?"

"There is NO WAY I am going to wear a costume with a CAT in it. That is dangerous!"

"Okay, Jadie," Mom said. "I have another idea we could try." She took an old rag and cut two little holes in the middle. "You can be a scary ghost," she said. I did NOT look scary at all.

Mom looked in her craft box for costume ideas.

"How about this?" she asked. She pulled some red netting out of the box. "I can make you a pretty red tutu and you can be a ballerina for Halloween."

She went to work making a beautiful red ballerina tutu.

I really liked it, until I tried it on...

"This costume is pretty, but very itchy," I thought. "My wings itch, and I cannot move them."

"I am not giving up yet, Jadie," said Mom.

She looked in a box of old troll dolls that she kept in the closet for when her grandchildren came over to play. She took one of the little dolls out of the box.

"This costume should fit you," Mom said. "You could be a cute little chef."

I tried on the little chef costume. "I like the hat," I thought, "but I cannot fit my wings through the sleeves. This just does not feel right."

Mom would not give up. She took the clothes from another troll doll in the box. "I think this witch costume is going to be perfect for you," she said.

I was going to wear the witch costume, but I ate the broom.

(I could not help it. It was tasty.)

"We are running out of time, Jadie," Mom said. "We must find a costume soon!"

I was getting worried. If Mom did not find a costume for me, I could not go trick or tweeting at school with all the children. I really wanted to go!

Mom thought and thought...

Mom smiled. "I have a GREAT idea!" she said. "YOU can be a part of MY costume, Jadie! I will go to my closet and put on our costume. I will be right back," she said.

I waited on top of my cage while Mom ran to her bedroom closet to get our costume. "What kind of costume could a big human share with a little green parrot?" I wondered.

"Close your eyes, Jadie," Mom said. "I want you to be surprised."

I closed my eyes.

(I was excited, but I kept them closed.)

"Now, hop on my shoulder. Be careful, hold on tight."

I hopped on Mom's shoulder.

"Are you peeking?" Mom asked.

"No, Mom," I thought.

(I really wanted to peek.)

"I am going to give you a ride to the mirror. Do NOT open your eyes until I tell you."

I hung on to Mom's shoulder, as she gave me a ride to the big mirror in her bedroom.

"Ready?" she asked.

COME ON, MOM!

"Okay," Mom said. "Open your eyes at the count of three."

"One...two...three!"

I opened my eyes, and...

"I will be a crusty old pirate, and YOU will be my trusty Parrot First Mate!" she laughed.
"I can do that!" I agreed. We finally found the PERFECT costume, just in time for Halloween.

Mom took me to school for the Halloween party. All the children at Mom's school wanted to meet me. I was excited, but a little nervous. I can be shy around new people, especially little squeaky people.

I stayed on top of Mom's shoulder for the whole day. I felt safe up there. The children said nice things about our costume. A little girl in a witch costume smiled at me and said I was very cute. She did not have a broom. I wondered if she ate her broom, too? Brooms are very tasty.

I saw lots of witches, ghosts, vampires, and monsters, but I was not afraid of any of them. I am a very brave Parrot First Mate.

There was this one costume that was VERY scary, though.

This was Mom's favorite costume.
I liked it, too.

This was my favorite costume.
She was a very purt-gurrrl, just like me!

Trick or tweeting was very fun, but I was the only one doing any tweeting. The teachers were all very nice. They passed out candy to the children even though they forgot to tweet.

The school children asked if they could share their candy with me, but Mom said, "No, thank you. Chocolate can make a parrot very sick."

Too bad for me.

I still had a great time at the Halloween party, even without any tweets. I like Halloween!

"Well, Jadie," Mom asked. "Would you like to come to school for Halloween again next year?"

I thought and thought...Yes, I would like to come next year, but I want to be a princess!

The End

CPSIA information can be obtained
at www.ICGtesting.com
Printed in the USA
BVHW020842200221
600617BV00008BA/1

9 780578 841588